ACKNOWLEDGMENTS

We would like to express our appreciation to the staff and volunteers of the Maturango Museum in Ridgecrest, California, for their cooperation on this project, and in particular we thank Edna Laytart for her excellent guidance in Little Petroglyph Canyon. We also thank NAWS at China Lake for permitting us to view the petroglyphs. In addition, we thank David S. Whitley, Institute of Archeology, Rock Art Archives, UCLA, Los Angeles, California, for his expert advice; and Joan Hewett, Arthur Arnold, and Matthew Arnold for their assistance with the photographs.

Photo credits:
pages 7, 14–15, 27, 43 *left*—Matthew Arnold; pages 22, 35—Arthur Arnold

Clarion Books
a Houghton Mifflin Company imprint
215 Park Avenue South, New York, NY 10003

The text for this book is set in 13/18-point Kuenstler.

For information about this and other Houghton Mifflin trade and reference books
and multimedia products, visit The Bookstore at Houghton Mifflin
on the World Wide Web at (http://www.hmco.com/trade/).

Printed in Hong Kong

Library of Congress Cataloging-in-Publication Data

Arnold, Caroline.
Stories in stone : rock art pictures by early Americans / by Caroline Arnold ;
photographs by Richard Hewett.
p.   cm.
Includes bibliographical references and index.
ISBN 0-395-72091-5
1. Indians of North America—California—Coso Range—Antiquities—Juvenile literature.
2. Petroglyphs—California—Coso Range—Juvenile literature.
3. Coso Range (Calif.)—Antiquities—Juvenile literature.
I. Hewett, Richard.   II. Title.
E78.C15A79   1996
709'.01'130979487—dc20   96-387
CIP
AC

DNP   10   9   8   7   6   5   4   3   2   1

Title page: A petroglyph depicting the body of a bighorn sheep penetrated by a spear.

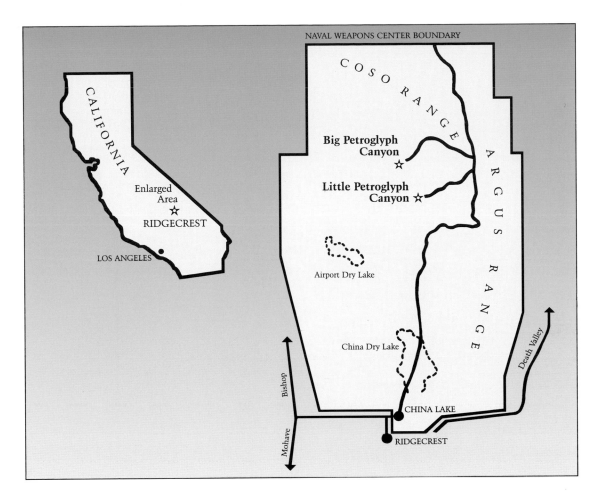

CONTENTS

Discovering Rock Art   4

Making Petroglyphs   12

The Earliest Americans   20

Ancient Hunters   27

Who Made the Coso Petroglyphs and Why?   36

Rock Art of North America   46

Glossary   47

Index   48

DISCOVERING ROCK ART

More than a thousand years ago a Native American artist crossed a mountain plateau in the Coso Range of eastern California. Passing campsites where hunters had built fires and shaped stone tools, this early American finally came to a narrow canyon where centuries of rushing water had exposed the broad vertical surfaces of the steep stone walls. The artist descended into the canyon and began to chip a line into one of the rocks with a stone tool. As the dark outer layer of the rock dropped away, the lighter-colored stone underneath began to reveal a design.

This drawing, along with thousands more on boulders nearby, can still be seen today. Some of the drawings are at least six thousand years old and may be much older. Others were made just a few hundred years ago. The drawings provide evidence of some of the earliest human habitation in the Americas. They also give us clues to what life may have been like for the people who once lived in these mountains and valleys of western North America.

Ancient images seem as fresh today as when they were carved hundreds of years ago.

4

Richly decorated panels like this are typical of the Cosos.

The Coso Range is about two hundred miles northeast of Los Angeles. It is one of a series of mountain ranges located in the northern Mojave Desert between Death Valley to the east and the Sierra Nevada mountains to the west. Narrow canyons cut across the broad tablelands below the peaks of the Cosos. During most of the year the streambeds at the bottom of the canyons are dry, and you can walk along them to view the art on the canyon walls. On some rocks there are rows of fat sheep following each other across the stony landscape. On others there are leaping deer and pouncing dogs or mountain lions. Some show human figures with rectangular bodies and elaborate head-dresses. Many drawings are abstract designs whose meaning is unknown. The drawings range in size from tiny figures a few inches high to huge, almost life-size images.

A small circle of stones is all that remains of an ancient Coso campsite.

The canyons of the Cosos contain more than 100,000 examples of rock art. This is the richest concentration of rock art in the Western Hemisphere. The drawings of the Cosos are part of an artistic tradition practiced by Native Americans who lived in the Great Basin, the broad inland area located between the Sierra Nevada and Rocky mountains. Some of the same images can be seen at other places in this region, but nowhere else is there such an abundance of drawings. The rock art of the Coso Range is unique both because of the huge number of drawings and because the site was used continuously for thousands of years.

People who study ancient cultures are called archeologists. They try to learn how people once lived by examining what they left behind. In the Coso region, archeologists have found house rings, hunting blinds, rock shelters, tool-making sites, grinding stones, and other indications of ancient life. But by far the most numerous and widespread signs of the people who once lived there are the rock drawings that dot the landscape.

Along the nine-mile length of Little Petroglyph Canyon there are more than 6000 examples of rock art. The walls of the canyon become nearly 300 feet high at its south end.

Rock art is one of the oldest known forms of human expression and can be seen at many sites throughout the world. Perhaps the most famous examples are the cave paintings of southern France and northern Spain. Those drawings of mammoths, horses, and other animals may be nearly 30,000 years old. Other notable ancient rock-art sites are found in the Sahara Desert, South Africa, and Australia.

Most North American rock art is found in the western United States, but examples can be seen in almost every state and in Canada and Mexico. The first scientific study of North American rock art was made in 1886 by Colonel Garrick Mallery of the United States Army, who was fascinated by what he called "Indian picture writing." Many more rock-art sites have been discovered in this century, but little work has been done to decipher their meaning. The main problem with interpreting the art is that in many cases we do not know exactly who made it.

This basket, made about 1950, is woven in the typical Shoshone style.

When ranchers and miners came to the Cosos in the 1800s they found Native Americans of the Panamint Shoshone tribe living in the area. (*Coso* is a Shoshone word meaning "fire.") The Shoshone were familiar with the images carved in the canyon walls of the Cosos but they had no knowledge of their meaning. The tradition of making rock art was no longer practiced and had been long forgotten. According to the Shoshone, the rock pictures had been made by the "old ones" who lived long ago. Most experts believe that the "old ones" were ancestors of the Shoshone. One way that archeologists determine how and when people came to different parts of North America is by looking at similarities in the languages that Native Americans speak today. These similarities reflect common roots. The Shoshone of the Cosos share ancestors with other Native Americans in the Great Basin and with people as far away as the Aztecs in Mexico.

Above: At Little Petroglyph Canyon the altitude is about 5000 feet above sea level, which makes the climate slightly cooler than that on the desert floor in the valley below.

Below: A replica of a petroglyph stands near the entrance to the Maturango Museum.

The main concentrations of rock art in the Cosos are at Big Petroglyph Canyon, Little Petroglyph Canyon (also called Renegade Canyon), Sheep Canyon, and Horse Canyon. In 1964, Little Petroglyph Canyon was listed in the National Register of Historic Places in recognition of its importance to our cultural heritage.

The term *rock art* includes drawings that are carved or engraved into stone as well as those that are painted on rock surfaces. Almost all of the drawings in the Cosos are engraved and most people refer to them as *petroglyphs,* a term that comes from the Greek words *petro* meaning "stone" and *glyph* meaning "letter" or "picture." Some people use the term *petroglyph* for a drawing that is cut into stone and the term *petrograph* for a drawing that is painted on stone. Others call paintings on stone *pictographs.* Because these terms are often confused, many experts prefer to use the term *rock art* for any kind of drawing that is made on a stone surface.

The entire Coso Range and the rock art in it are within the China Lake United States Naval Air Weapons Station (NAWS), which maintains and protects the site. The Cosos became part of NAWS in the 1940s. Before that a few hardy ranchers and miners worked the land. Today, wild horses and burros roam the high ranges where those people once lived.

Arrangements for visits to Little Petroglyph Canyon can be made at the Maturango Museum in Ridgecrest, California. Museum staff and volunteers guide visitors through the canyon and help them to understand the art and surrounding landscape. You can also learn about the petroglyphs and the people who made them by viewing exhibits at the museum. Visits to the petroglyphs are made mainly during the late spring and early fall months. In summer the heat is intense, and in winter rain often turns to snow and the roads through the mountains are closed.

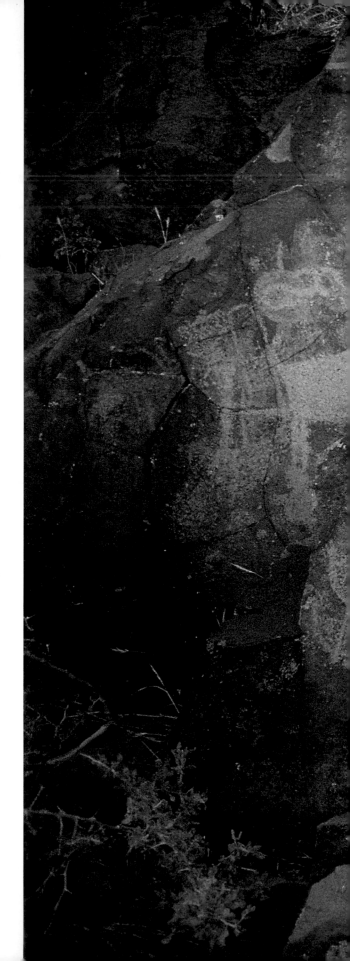

MAKING PETROGLYPHS

The petroglyph artists of the Cosos used several methods to create their designs. In some cases they used a sharp rock as a knife to cut a line into the rock surface. By making repeated cuts, they deepened the lines into grooves. Other designs were made by pecking small pits into the rock surface. The artist either held a pointed stone and hit the rock surface with it directly or placed the pointed stone on the surface and used another rock as a hammer to hit it. A series of pecked dots were often joined to make a line. The pecking technique was also used to fill in areas of a drawing and create the appearance of a solid shape. Another way to expose a large area was to use a flat-edged stone to scrape away the dark surface. In some cases, artists used several techniques in the same drawing.

The creation of a petroglyph was a slow and painstaking process. Most experts believe that only a few new drawings were made each year in the canyons of the Cosos. The huge number of petroglyphs located there is the accumulation of many centuries of work.

Rock art is frequently found along trails or near sources of water.

Most of the petroglyphs in the Cosos are drawn on basalt, a hard, light-colored rock formed by volcanic action within the earth. The rocks used most often for petroglyphs in North America were basalt, sandstone, and granite. All of these rocks develop a dark surface, or *patina,* when exposed to the weather for a long period of time. It is not known exactly how the patina forms, but it occurs in desert regions where high summer temperatures combine with periodic rain showers. When water falls on the sun-heated rock it causes a chemical reaction that darkens the surface. Often the wind scours the patina with fine dust or sand, and the resulting shiny brown or blue-black surface is known as "desert varnish." Rocks stained by minerals or blackened with smoke also made good surfaces for petroglyphs.

The light-colored rock of a newly drawn petroglyph gradually turns dark again over time. Thus, dark drawings are likely to be older than those that are light.

The dark patina on the rock's surface makes a dramatic background for the design chipped into the light-colored rock underneath.

15

The oldest drawings in the Cosos are abstract designs. These deeply cut drawings depict lines, circles, grids, and other shapes. Many of these old drawings are located at the north end of Little Petroglyph Canyon. On some you can see colorful lichen, a small growth that clings to rocky surfaces. Lichens develop extremely slowly, sometimes increasing less than a millimeter a year. Heavy lichen growth on a petroglyph suggests that it is older than one with less lichen.

The deep grooves of some of these designs suggest that they may have been reworked over a period of years.

16

Many sites in the Cosos were used repeatedly over a long period of time. Some rocks have dozens of drawings, often superimposed on one another with those on the top being newer than those underneath. The sequence of drawings helps us to understand how styles and designs changed over time. For instance, sheep in older drawings tend to have rounded bodies, whereas sheep in the newer drawings have bodies that are more boat shaped.

Drawing styles, subject matter, and the amount of desert varnish or lichen growth help give a rough idea of a petroglyph's age, but they are not accurate measurements. A more precise method that scientists use to determine the age of ancient objects is called *radiocarbon dating.* Anything composed of living or once-living material contains the element carbon. Over long periods of time the carbon gives off tiny amounts of radioactivity at a regular rate. Scientists can measure the radioactivity and determine the age of the object within a few hundred years. Rocks are not composed of living material and ordinarily do not lend themselves to radiocarbon dating. However, in some petroglyphs scientists have found small pieces of algae and other living matter trapped between the rock surface and the layer of varnish that formed after the petroglyphs were made. The radiocarbon dates of these samples suggest that some of the petroglyphs underneath were made at least 16,000 to 18,000 years ago. If this is true, then they would help establish that people were living in western North America much earlier than previously thought.

The newer designs obscure those that are underneath.

Hunters pursue bison in this diorama.

THE EARLIEST AMERICANS

Most experts believe that the first humans came to North America from Asia sometime during the last Ice Age, which began about 100,000 years ago and ended about 11,000 years ago. At several points during that time, so much of the earth's water was frozen in huge glaciers that the oceans were several hundred feet lower than they are today. At the Bering Strait between Alaska and Asia a land bridge connected the two continents, and people could walk across. From there they continued southward, eventually reaching the tip of South America.

The oldest firmly dated human-made objects known in North America are several stone spearheads called Clovis points that were found near Clovis,

New Mexico. These are about 11,300 years old. However, people probably came to North American much earlier than that. Recent discoveries at a cave in Pennsylvania and at two sites in South America suggest that people may have migrated to the Americas as long as 30,000 years ago.

Most experts agree that people were living in California at least 10,000 to 15,000 years ago. Archeologists call these people Paleo-Indians. The Paleo-Indians were nomadic hunters, moving about in small groups in pursuit of large animals such as mammoths, giant bison, and camels. Armed with stone-tipped spears, they followed their prey across the land. After a successful hunt, they used the fresh meat for food, the skins for clothing, and the bones for making tools. Paleo-Indians also gathered fruits, nuts, roots, and other plant foods to supplement their diet.

Life for early humans in North America was both difficult and dangerous. Ancient hunters had to compete for prey with other large predators such as sabertooth cats and lions. And because they had no permanent settlements, they were always at the mercy of the elements.

Stone spear points such as these were used by ancient hunters.

Obsidian chips found in the Cosos are remnants of ancient tool making.

21

At the end of the Ice Age, the shallow water of receding lakes provided places for ancient Americans to hunt for fish, waterfowl, and other aquatic life.

During the Ice Age, the climate in North America was cooler and wetter than it is today. The northern part of the continent was covered by thick ice, and in places that are now desert, huge herds of animals roamed across grassy plains. In eastern California a series of deep lakes filled the valleys between the mountains. One of these was China Lake, now a dry lakebed at the foot of the Cosos. Wild horses, camels, and elephant-like mastodons grazed at the lake's edge, and huge birds soared in the blue sky above.

22

Beginning about 10,000 years ago, the climate became warmer and drier. As small sources of water gradually disappeared, the large lakes of eastern California became magnets for both human and animal life. Archeologists have found the remains of a 10,000-year-old village at the edge of what once was China Lake. The climate continued to grow hotter and drier, and by about 6000 years ago many of the large animal species such as mammoths, camels, and horses became extinct. Although hunting by humans may have hastened the extinction of large animals in North America, the shortage of food and water that resulted from the changing climate also made it difficult for the animals to survive. What had been a hospitable landscape in eastern California during the Ice Age turned into one of the hottest, driest places on earth, the Mojave Desert.

As the lakes of the Ice Age dried up, they often left a flaky mineral crust.

When the Paleo-Indian period ended, about 6000–5000 B.C., a new way of life called the Archaic period began. It focused on hunting small game and collecting various wild plants. The Archaic people were semi-nomadic and migrated with the changing seasons. In the deserts of California, they moved into the foothills of the mountains each spring in search of new plant foods; they went to the mountains in late summer to harvest acorns and other seeds and fruits. Deer and sheep were hunted in the fall. When cold winter weather came to the mountains the people moved back to their villages on the valley floor and lived on food they had collected and stored.

During the Archaic period some people left eastern California and moved east into the Four Corners region, the place where Arizona, New Mexico, Utah, and Colorado now meet. About 2000 years ago, they began to grow corn and squash and settled into larger, more permanent communities. Archeologists call these people the Basket Makers because of their finely made baskets. Later their culture developed into that of the Anasazi and other groups.

Small caves provided temporary shelter on seasonal expeditions by Native Americans who lived in the deserts of eastern California.

In the deserts of eastern California, the harsh climate did not lend itself to farming. The people of the Coso region did not establish large permanent settlements like those of Native Americans in the Southwest. They continued to live a semi-nomadic life based on hunting and gathering wild foods.

Like early Americans elsewhere, the people of the Cosos used baskets for cooking and for storing water and food.

These mortar holes, sunk into the bedrock on the rim of Little Petroglyph Canyon, were used for grinding seeds and nuts into meal.

Above: Dogs may have helped hunters to chase sheep.

ANCIENT HUNTERS

Many of the Coso petroglyphs depict hunters, weapons, or animals being pursued by hunters. Hunters are usually drawn as stick figures and often carry weapons. The hunters most often are shown as single figures or in small groups, but on one panel there is a line of more than a hundred figures marching toward a group of sheep. This drawing may represent a large hunting party or perhaps a migration.

Mountain sheep and deer were the most commonly hunted large animals in the Cosos. Meat was also provided by lizards, birds, rabbits, and other small animals that were snared or trapped in nets. In addition to sheep, animals depicted in the Coso petroglyphs include deer, mountain lions, coyotes, foxes, lizards, snakes, tortoises, and quail.

Left: Petroglyph of ancient hunter holding a spear.

An atlatl helped a hunter to hurl his spear with more force.

Notches in stones were used to straighten the wooden shafts of ancient spears.

The Coso petroglyphs reflect how hunting techniques in North America changed over the years. The first hunters used long spears to kill large animals. Then, about 10,000 years ago or possibly earlier, they began to use a device called an *atlatl*. This was a short stick, usually about two feet long, that helped hurl the spear harder and farther than before. One end of the atlatl was attached by a hook to the back end of a spear and the other end was held in the hand. A hunter grasped the atlatl and the spear, swung his arm forward, and released the spear. Aborigines in Australia today use similar throwing sticks. With them they can hurl spears nearly four hundred feet, or more than three times the distance that a spear can be thrown without a throwing stick.

Atlatls, spear shafts, and spear points have been found at numerous sites in the Americas. Often the atlatls have small stones with them. A stone weight fastened to the center of the atlatl increased the force of the throw. Hunters may also have added small stones as charms for good luck. In the petroglyphs of the Cosos, atlatls are portrayed frequently. Often they are drawn bigger than life and with greatly enlarged stone weights.

In these petroglyphs of atlatls the stone weights are greatly enlarged.

The back of the sheep on the left has been pierced by an arrow.

Between 2500 and 2000 years ago, the bow and arrow appeared in the Coso region and gradually replaced the atlatl as the weapon of choice. Bows and arrows were much lighter for hunters to carry, were more accurate, had a longer range, and allowed a hunter to remain concealed longer when stalking prey. Because atlatls were no longer in use after about A.D. 300, petroglyphs of atlatls are believed to have been made earlier than that.

Above: In this unusual petroglyph, the hunters seem to be aiming their arrows at one another. No other Coso petroglyphs indicate combat or warfare.

Right: The bow and arrow made it easier to stalk deer. Although deer were common prey for ancient hunters, relatively few deer are depicted in the canyons of the Cosos.

31

This deeply grooved sheep is nearly life-size.

The most popular subject of ancient rock artists both in the Cosos and at many other sites in the western United States was the bighorn sheep. In Little Petroglyph Canyon alone there are more than 7000 depictions of sheep. In some cases the sheep are represented only by a pair of horns or by heads, but most are full body profiles. Often they are drawn in groups, sometimes with hunters and other animals. In one instance a small sheep is drawn inside the body of a larger animal, possibly depicting a pregnant ewe.

Sheep are almost always depicted with their bodies in profile, but their horns were drawn from either the front or the side; heads are sometimes shown facing front.

These sheep were pecked over earlier designs.

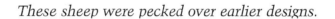

Bighorn, or mountain, sheep are found in high, rocky areas throughout western North America. They are excellent climbers and can move quickly along steep slopes. These large animals, which weigh up to 275 pounds, are distinguished by their massive, curving horns. The horns are larger in males than in females and can weigh as much as twenty pounds each. For many ancient Americans, the bighorn sheep was a source of meat as well as hides, sinew, bone, and horn.

The canyons of the Cosos would have been a good place to trap bands of sheep because the steep walls made it hard for the sheep to escape. At several places in the canyons there are rock barriers that may be ancient "blinds" where hunters hid while waiting for sheep to pass by. In a few places there are also rocks that have been piled like snowmen on the canyon rim. At a distance they look something like people and may have been built to fool sheep into going down into the canyon toward waiting hunters.

Today the desert bighorn sheep is endangered due to hunting and loss of its natural habitat.

Ancient hunters may have trapped sheep in natural corrals such as this.

One of the mysteries of the Coso petroglyphs is why hunting themes are so dominant, especially in the more recently made designs. Most of the sheep and hunting scenes appear to have been made during the last 1500 years, a period when it is known that meat was decreasing in importance as a source of food for people in the Coso region. Instead, people there had begun to rely more heavily on plant foods such as pine nuts, which were collected each fall from mountain forests. They also irrigated native plants to help them grow more productively. The climate had grown drier, and there were fewer large animals to hunt than in earlier times. It is possible that the Coso petroglyphs were associated with some sort of hunting rituals, perhaps to bestow luck upon the hunters before a hunt or to record a successful hunt. It is more likely, however, that the drawings are symbols associated with religious or ceremonial practices.

WHO MADE THE COSO PETROGLYPHS AND WHY?

There is no historical record of petroglyph-making in the Cosos. With no direct evidence of who made the petroglyphs or why they did so, it is hard to know for certain exactly what they mean. On the other hand, experts believe that the people of the Cosos shared many customs and beliefs with other Native American groups in the region. Those beliefs and practices provide some clues to the significance of the ancient images. Many Native American groups in California made rock art. Rocks or caves were believed to be entrances to the spiritual world, and rock-art sites were thought to be places with special power.

Human figures are the second most commonly drawn design in the Cosos.

The interpretation of the Coso petroglyphs varies considerably, but most experts believe that they were created as part of religious rituals. As in other Native American cultures, these rituals would have been performed by a shaman, or medicine man. (Most shamans were men, although women could also be shamans.)

A shaman was the village leader and played an important role in the community. His duties included foretelling the future, finding lost objects, curing sickness, controlling the weather, guiding souls to the afterlife, and locating food sources. It was the shaman's responsibility to communicate with the spiritual world on behalf of the community. The shaman was believed to have the ability to bring the power of the spirits to the people. A shaman entered the spiritual world by going into a trance or a dream. One way that he communicated what he had seen in his vision was by painting or carving the images on stone. In some Native American languages the word that means "shaman" also means "a man who writes on rocks." Most of the petroglyphs of the Cosos were probably made by shamans either as interpretations of their visions or as part of other religious activities.

The Coso petroglyphs feature a wide variety of human or godlike figures, and experts believe that they represent shamans. The figures often have headdresses and fringed clothing, and some appear to wear ear ornaments or carry weapons. Their rectangular bodies (which are sometimes interpreted as shields) are decorated with crosshatching, diamond shapes, dots, zigzags, and other patterns. In some cases, the figures are part human and part animal.

This shaman appears to wear a cap decorated with a quail feather.

It was believed that spirit helpers, which often took the form of animals, accompanied the shaman to the spirit world. In Native American cultures of the Great Basin area, one of the most important spirit helpers was the bighorn sheep. In particular, the bighorn sheep helped a shaman to control the weather by influencing the bringing of wind, thunder, lightning, and rain. It was believed that rain would fall when a mountain sheep was killed.

Petroglyphs of purselike shapes are often called medicine bags. It is not known whether this is what they actually represent.

Joshua trees thrive on the high desert mesas of the Cosos. They get needed moisture from winter snows and occasional summer thunderstorms.

In a desert region such as the Cosos, rain was essential for the growth of the plants that provided most of the people's food. The pictures of sheep and hunting scenes may have been drawn as part of rituals to control the weather. Instead of actually killing a sheep in an effort to bring rain, the shaman may have carved a picture of a sheep on a rock. The large number of sheep in the canyons of the Cosos suggests that this site was a center for rainmaking shamanism. Shamans who specialized in the control of weather used ceremonial objects such as sheep horns and dried sheep meat and fat. They also wore caps and belts made of sheepskin.

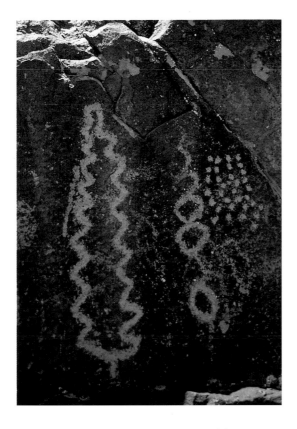 

In addition to recognizable images on the rocks of the Cosos, there are thousands of abstract designs. Some resemble suns, clouds, nets, or flowing water, but others are impossible to decipher. They may have been made in connection with rituals regarding the change of seasons or astronomical events. In other places in California it is known that people made rock art as part of the celebration of the winter solstice, the shortest day of the year. Some rock art has symbols that are associated with fertility rites. Drawings with repeated dots or lines suggest counting systems or tabulations. Others resemble maps, and some may tell stories or record special events. The world of ancient Native Americans was complex, and in many cases we will never know for sure what the objects represented in rock art mean.

Above and left: The meaning of many petroglyph designs is up to the viewer's imagination.

Before there was paper for drawing or canvas for painting, ancient artists turned to nature's rock walls for surfaces on which to create their art. Many of the images appear as fresh today as when they were drawn hundreds or even thousands of years ago. Rock art is one of the oldest and most permanent art forms and provides a fascinating glimpse into the past.

The Coso petroglyphs are the enduring legacy of ancient Americans who walked the canyons of eastern California. They have been preserved in remarkably good condition because of the dry desert climate, the remote and inhospitable nature of the region, and the restricted access. The stories recorded by these ancient images in stone are yet untold and may never be known. Even so, we can appreciate their beauty and mystery and wonder about the people who made them centuries ago.

A herd of sheep, trapped in time, march across a rocky landscape.

45

Petroglyph at Dinosaur National Monument, Utah.

ROCK ART OF NORTH AMERICA

You can find rock art in many parts of North America. Many of the designs are engraved on rocks, but others are painted in brilliant black, white, or red pigments. In a few places you can also see giant figures called geoglyphs that were created by scraping pebbles off the ground to leave the shape of people or animals. Ranging from highly abstract to clearly recognizable images, the rock art of North America represents an artistic tradition begun in ancient times and practiced for thousands of years.

Here are a few places where you can see rock art.

Canyon de Chelly, Arizona (Spanish horseman)
Petrified Forest, Arizona ("Newspaper Rock")
Blythe, California (giant geoglyph figures)
Joshua Tree National Monument, California (red painted designs)
Lava Beds National Monument, California (abstract designs)
Ridgecrest, California (Little Petroglyph Canyon)
Mesa Verde National Park, Colorado (animals and figure)
Manistique, Michigan (headless figure)
Washington State Park, Missouri (abstract symbols)
Dinosaur National Monument, Utah (figures)
Zion National Park, Utah (row of human figures)
Horsethief Lake State Park, Washington (large face)
Olympic National Park, Washington (killer whales)

GLOSSARY

Anasazi—a Native American culture of the Southwest that began about A.D. 1 and existed until A.D. 1300 or later.

Archaic—period of human history in western North America between the Paleo-Indian and Basket Maker periods.

archeology—the study of any prehistoric culture by excavation and description of its remains.

atlatl—a wooden spear-throwing stick used by ancient hunters; *atlatl* is an Aztec word.

basalt—a light-colored rock formed by volcanic action.

Basket Maker period—the span of Native American culture of the Southwest from about A.D. 1–550.

bighorn sheep—large wild animals with curved horns that inhabit high, rocky terrain in western North America; also called mountain sheep.

Clovis point—a stone spear point or knife 4–12 centimeters long; most are about 11,000–12,000 years old.

Coso Range—California mountain range west of Death Valley.

culture—a people's activities as well as their clothes, food, dwellings, and beliefs.

desert bighorn sheep—a subspecies of bighorn sheep that lives in mountainous desert regions.

desert varnish—the shiny surface created when wind and sand scour the patina on a rock.

geoglyph—ground figure made by the removal of surface gravel to expose the lighter soil underneath.

Great Basin—the region between the Rocky Mountains and the Sierra Nevada.

hunting blind—a barrier for hunters to hide behind while waiting for prey.

Ice Age—the geologic period from about 100,000 to 10,000 years ago when much of the earth's surface was covered in ice.

lichen—a plant without stem or leaves, consisting of algae and fungi growing in close association.

Mojave—desert region in eastern California.

mortar—a bowl or a bowl-like hole in stone or wood in which food can be ground or pounded with a pestle.

obsidian—natural volcanic glass; it was the most common material for stone-tipped tools in California.

Paleo-Indians—nomadic hunter-gatherers who lived in the Americas before 6000 B.C.

Panamint Shoshone—the branch of the Shoshone group that lives in the Coso region of California.

patina—the dark coloring on the surface of a rock that results from weathering.

pestle—a long stone or wood pounding tool used to pulverize food products in a mortar.

petroglyph—a drawing made on stone, usually unpainted.

petrograph—a drawing made on stone.

pictograph—a picture used as a word or symbol; sometimes refers to painted rock art.

plateau—a high, flat land.

radiocarbon dating—the measurement of radioactivity to determine the age of ancient objects made of living material.

rock art—any design made on stone surfaces by humankind.

shaman—a Native American religious leader or "medicine man."

Shoshone—Native American tribe found in the Great Basin area.

Sierra Nevada—the high mountain range in California that forms the western border of the Great Basin.

spirit helpers—animals or other beings that were believed to aid a shaman on his journeys to the spirit world.